OTTO'S TRUNK

Sandy Turner

JOANNA COTLER BOOKS
An Imprint of HarperCollins Publishers

Otto's Trunk

Copyright © 2003 by Sandy Turner

Manufactured in China. All rights reserved.

www.harperchildrens.com

Library of Congress

Cataloging-in-Publication Data is available.

ISBN 0-06-000956-X

ISBN 0-06-000957-8 (lib. bdg.)

Typography by Alicia Mikles

1 2 3 4 5 6 7 8 9 10

First Edition

Otto wasn't very happy about his trunk. Everyone else thought it was a hoot!

The herd thought it was hilarious.

They suggested that Otto could get employment in a circus sideshow . . . right next to the bearded lady maybe.

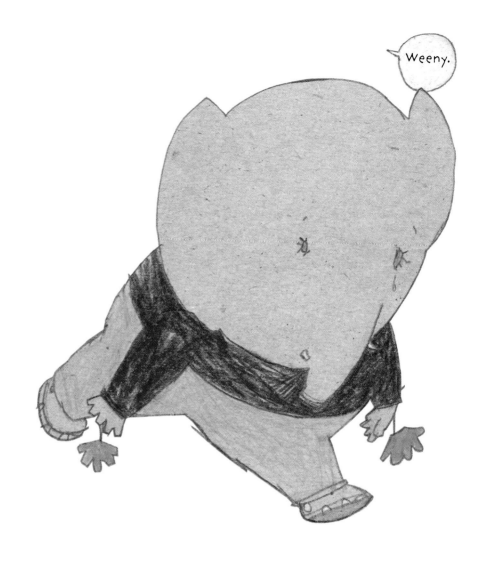

Otto retreated for a period of reflection and meditation.

After about two minutes, when no one was around, when no one was looking . . .

... Otto tried out ways to improve his trunk.

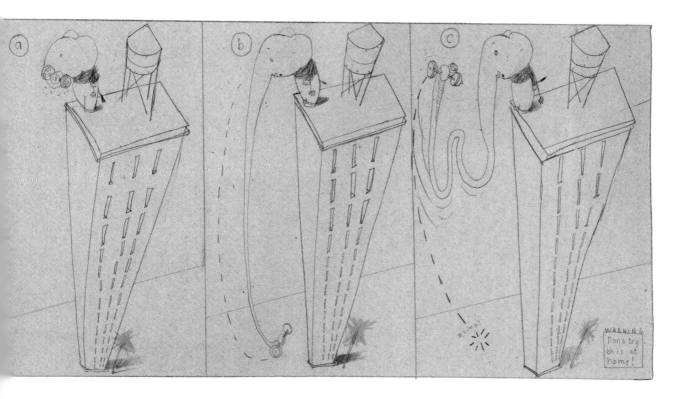

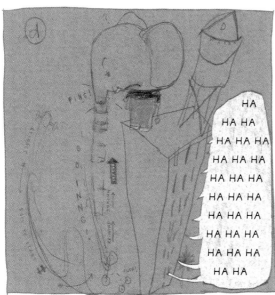

But all he ended up with was a sore trunk.

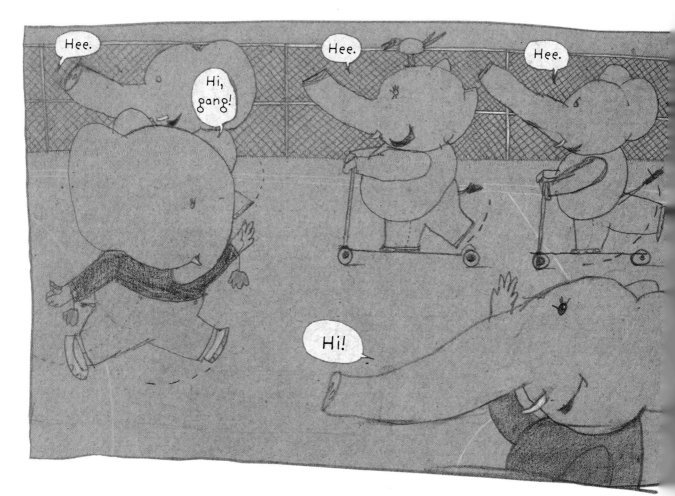

The next day (Tuesday) . . .

... it started up again.

Squirt!

At this moment
(11 A.M. on Tuesday),
Otto felt as if the
whole world was
laughing at his
trunk.

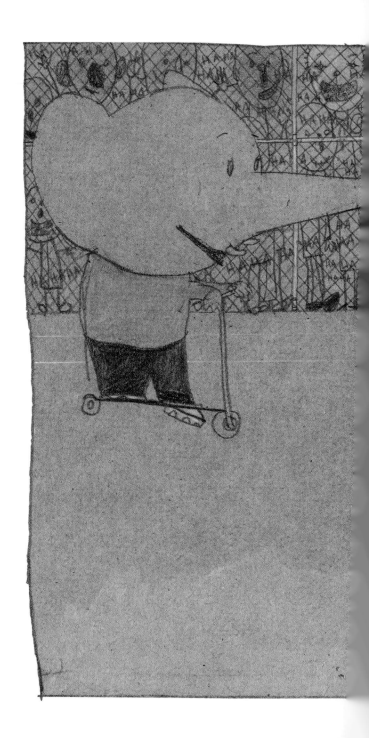

. . . I want one just like my dad's.

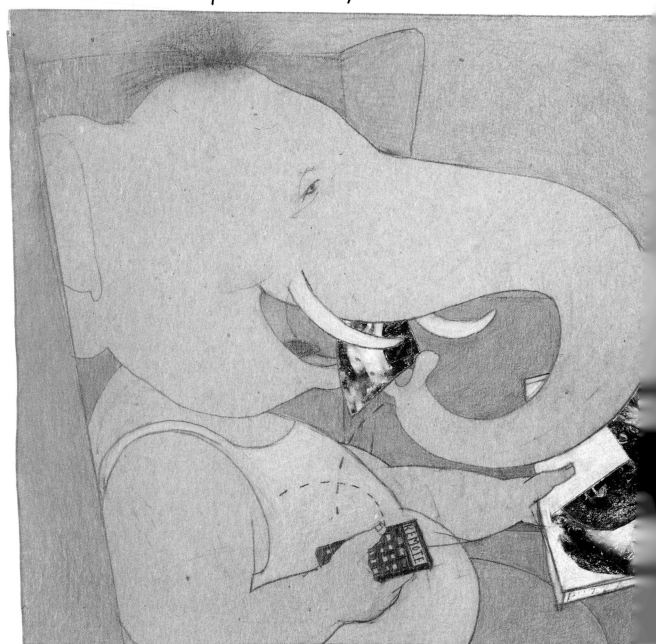

The next day (Wednesday),
Otto met up with the herd as usual.

And Friday arrived. Still the herd
hooted and laughed.

And then Otto snorted. At first it was just an ordinary snort. But it grew in volume until it became . . .

a snort that
roared,

hissed,

hogged,

mooed,

and
cock-a-doodle
dooed!

The next day (Saturday).